24

INVASION OF THE
BRAIN SHARPENERS

Invasion of the BrainSharpeners

by PHILIP CURTIS
illustrated by Tony Ross

ALFRED A. KNOPF ★ NEW YORK

THIS IS A BORZOI BOOK
PUBLISHED BY ALFRED A. KNOPF, INC.

First U.S. Edition, 1981
Text Copyright © 1979 by Philip Curtis
Illustrations Copyright © 1979 by Andersen Press Limited
Cover illustration by Tony Ross

Originally published in Great Britain as
Mr. Browser and the Brain Sharpeners by
Anderson Press Limited in association with
Hutchinson Limited, London.

Manufactured in the United States of America.
10   9   8   7   6   5   4   3   2

Library of Congress Cataloging in Publication Data
Curtis, Philip.
Invasion of the brain sharpeners.
(Capers)
Reprint of the ed. published by Andersen Press,
London under title: Mr. Browser and the brain sharpeners.
Summary: Extraterrestrial beings attempt to sharpen
the brains of a school class they wish to develop their
new planets. One child resists.
[1. Science fiction.   2. School stories]   I. Ross,
Tony.   II. Title.   III. Series.
PZ7.C9483In   [Fic]   80–21434
ISBN 0–394–84676–1 (pbk.)
ISBN 0–394–94676–6 (lib. bdg.)

Contents

INVASION OF THE
BRAIN SHARPENERS

1*

First Contact

The first contact with the Brain Sharp-eners was made on a foggy morning in February. But Michael Fairlie insists that Mr. Browser, the fifth-grade teacher, must have been in distant communication with them before that.

It seems that a few days earlier Michael had been standing by Mr. Browser's desk. As he half-listened to his teacher explain how to do long division, Anna Cardwell came over with a broken pencil. Anna is a round-faced girl with large, innocent-looking eyes. She's also one of

3

the class's champion pencil-point breakers—
especially when there's math to be done.

"Please, Mr. Browser," she began.

"Don't tell me, Anna. Your pencil's broken."

"Yes, Mr. Browser. Could you sharpen it for
me, please?"

Mr. Browser shook his head wearily as he
looked at the broken-off end. Then he took his
ancient penknife from his pocket and set to work

on the pencil. Mr. Browser's classroom didn't have a pencil sharpener. The old one had broken early in the year, and he kept forgetting to order a new one.

"How are you doing with the long division, Anna?" he asked.

"I don't think I really understand it, Mr. Browser," Anna answered honestly.

"Neither does Michael," said Mr. Browser. "If only I had a brain sharpener as well as a pencil sharpener, maybe we'd learn a little more quickly!"

Anna giggled. But Michael, who was looking at Mr. Browser's face, noticed that the teacher's eyes took on a glazed look as soon as he spoke the words "brain sharpener." In fact, Mr. Browser was staring into space as though listening to something far away.

("I thought he had indigestion," said Anna, when Michael asked her about it later. "He suddenly held the knife still and just stared. It was as if you and I and the rest of the class weren't there for him any more. After a few seconds, he clicked back into consciousness and gave me my pencil.")

"Brain sharpeners," said Mr. Browser, as though the idea appealed to him greatly. "We could certainly do with some for this class. Nice children, but they will not listen. I've said this before, Michael, haven't I?"

"Yes, Mr. Browser."

At least a hundred times—he's always saying it, thought Michael. He tried harder then to listen as Mr. Browser once more began explaining long division.

Several days passed before anything else unusual happened to Mr. Browser and his fifth-grade class. By that time Michael and Anna had completely forgotten their teacher's comment about brain sharpeners. Mr. Browser often made little jokes like that. They helped the mathematical medicine go down better for some of the class.

Monday was unusually foggy. Michael got to the playground at about 8:20 that morning. His mother started work very early on Mondays, and she always took Michael to school by car because Chivvy Chase School was on her way to work. And Michael was so forgetful and untidy—so she said—that she preferred to make sure he arrived at school in one piece.

So, on this foggy day Michael was quite early for school. He ran down the path to the playground, pretty sure that no one else would be there yet. He liked having the playground to himself so he could run without fear of being knocked over. He could also play marbles against himself with no danger of losing. Best of all, he could use the climbing equipment as he wished without upsetting anyone else.

Michael headed straight for the monkey bars and clambered up to the top. It was pleasant to sit there and look down on the empty playground and the deserted school. Even the precise principal, Mr. Salt, would not have arrived yet. His shining new car was usually the first one to arrive in the parking lot at about 8:30.

The fog had changed the usual scene completely. To his own surprise, Michael was a bit

7

uneasy as he sat and surveyed his kingdom. The fog seemed to be closing in on him. The houses at the side of the playground were completely hidden, and fog was swirling around the trash cans at the far end. He couldn't see the football posts in the middle of the school field. Even the school building itself was hazy.

For once, Michael wished someone else would show up. It would be good to hear another voice. The fog was dampening sounds and making the world a mysterious place. If only Spiky Jackson or Jason Little would come running across the playground!

It was cool at the top of the monkey bars, with the fog swirling around him. Michael began to consider what he might do when he climbed down to the playground again. He was about to drop to a lower bar when he thought he heard the wind blowing in from the direction of the field. He stopped and frowned. Wind and fog don't go together, he thought. Just then, all the fog on the field seemed to start blowing across toward him. Michael clung to the cold bars as the fog streamed past as if it were being puffed out by some giant smoker. He could hear a whirring sound, followed by a sudden plop and hiss.

For a second or two a gap opened up as the fog was blown away. Through the gap Michael saw a huge white thing with windows sitting in the middle of the school field. Then the fog closed in again, and the sudden wind died away.

Michael climbed down and walked to the edge of the field. As hard as he stared, there was

nothing to be seen but fog. He shivered—as much with excitement as with cold. The thing had looked almost like a huge pepperpot. The holes near the top of it were probably windows. Had a plane landed on the field? Michael didn't really want to think about it. But deep down he knew that either his eyes had deceived him or he had seen some kind of spacecraft. No airplane on earth resembled the object he had seen.

As far as he could tell, the playground was still deserted. If only someone would come, he could describe what he had seen. But would anyone believe him? Not a hope, Michael decided unhappily. He could hardly believe his own eyes! There was only one way to prove to himself that he had not been dreaming. He'd have to walk to the middle of the field and take another look. Michael put one foot on the grass, then withdrew it. To walk on the field before nine o'clock was to break one of the school's strictest rules. The field was very wet and muddy that morning, so Mr. Salt would be especially angry if Michael crossed it.

Excuses! If he didn't dare go out there, he would never know the truth. He might be missing the biggest sensation of the century! Michael looked around to make sure he was still alone. Then he courageously stepped off the pavement. He moved slowly over the grass, carefully looking and listening as he went.

Was that a faint ticking sound coming from the place where the thing had landed? Or was it just his imagination? Michael stopped, listened, and moved on again. Now the playground was no longer visible. He was lost in a sea of fog. There were no familiar buildings in sight. Michael was on his own with whatever might be out there on the football field.

Suddenly, there it was, hovering a few inches above the ground and ticking like an old grandfather clock. Swift rays of light shot out of it. Michael was caught in a tunnel of light that reached from the pepperpot to himself, and no farther.

He wanted to turn and run, but his feet would not obey him. As he stood there against his will,

a door in the side of the spaceship opened. Inside, he could see a collection of illuminated gadgets that looked like a huge computer system. A platform rose up just inside the doorway. On the platform was a miniature pepperpot. It was exactly the same shape as the big one, but it had a large opening in the front of it. The purpose of this was soon revealed to Michael.

"Boy," began a dry voice coming from the

hole in the little pepperpot, "you are in the class of Mr. Browser, are you not?"

"I am," replied Michael. The machine repeated his words in its harsh voice. Then followed a whirring and clicking. The machine was evidently translating the English into its own language. A pause, more whirrings, and the machine spoke again.

"Boy, inform Mr. Browser at once that the Brain Sharpeners have answered his call. Say that we want to see him. He must come at once. Tell no one else what you have seen out here. We are already reading your brain. We know before you speak exactly what you intend to say. If you are tempted to tell of what you have seen, be warned. We have the power to make you unconscious before the words can even leave your mouth. Now, go get your Mr. Browser."

"But he probably isn't here yet," protested Michael. He was trembling all over.

The little pepperpot whirred and clicked. "Go and wait for him," it said. "He is approaching the school gates now. Leave at once!"

The light from the big pepperpot died away, and the fog swirled around Michael once more. Now it was thicker than ever. Seconds later the big pepperpot was hidden completely.

2★

Mr. Browser Meets
the Brain Sharpeners

Michael turned and ran diagonally across the field. He was heading in what he thought was the direction of the parking lot. His sides were aching by the time the path around the school came into view, but he dared not stop. The only car parked in the lot was the principal's sleek Cadillac. Michael ran past it and down the drive toward the school gate.

Mr. Browser's old Chevy swung into the entrance just as Michael arrived there. The teacher braked sharply and wound down his window.

"Michael, what are you doing here? On a

foggy day like this, too! You're breaking the school rule. Worse than that, you're asking to be run over. Back you go to the playground at once!"

"But Mr. Browser! I've got a message for you. Somebody wants to see you."

"Come down to the parking lot then, Michael. I'll talk to you there. If we stop here, there might be an accident."

So Michael ran alongside the old car until Mr. Browser had parked it in its usual place.

"Now, boy," the teacher said, picking up his briefcase and climbing out of the car. "Who wants to see me so early in the morning? Mr. Salt?"

"No, Mr. Browser. There's something out there on the field, and it asked me to get you immediately!"

"*It?* What do you mean, *it?*"

"Well, it's a kind of spacecraft, I suppose you'd call it. Looks like a big pepperpot. And there's all sorts of computer instruments inside."

Mr. Browser stared at Michael.

16

"Look here, Michael Fairlie," he said. "It's only February twelfth, not April first. Stop trying to fool me. Were you watching a science fiction movie last night?"

"I'm not fooling you, sir, I'm not! Please Mr. Browser, I had to make sure you would come. Please go out on the field. Then you'll see for yourself that I'm telling the truth. They call themselves the Brain Sharpeners, Mr. Browser!"

17

"The Brain Sharpeners!" Something registered in Mr. Browser's mind. He stared hard again at Michael. The boy appeared to be trembling. "All right, Michael," he said. "I'll take a look. But if I don't find anything there, you can expect a hard day's work!"

"Yes, Mr. Browser. Over there, in the middle of the field."

"Aren't you coming with me?"

"Oh no, Mr. Browser. It's you they want to see. You alone," said Michael. He felt as though his words had been directed by some power beyond himself.

"Calm down, Michael. You'd better go back to the playground," said Mr. Browser, striding off into the fog.

As soon as his teacher had disappeared, Michael walked along the edge of the field to the playground. By this time, most of the other children had arrived.

"Where have you been, Michael?" his friend Jason Little asked. "What were you doing on the field? Your shoes are covered with mud!"

18

Michael hunted frantically to find some answers. He wanted to tell Jason about the pepperpot, but he dared not. He felt dizzy at the very thought of revealing the truth about the Brain Sharpeners.

"I've been chasing a sea gull on the football field," he said weakly. "It couldn't see me in the fog. I nearly caught it."

"You're crazy!" Jason said. "Come on. Let's play a game of marbles."

"It's too cold," objected Michael.

"Not as cold as standing there and staring into the fog," Jason retorted.

"Oh, leave me alone!"

"All right, I will!"

Jason found it hard to believe that his friend meant what he said. When it became obvious that Michael really did mean it, Jason ran off to find some more friendly companions. Michael was left staring out into the fog, listening hard for any of the strange sounds he had heard earlier.

All was quiet on the field, but there was plenty of noise coming from the children in the playground. Now and again his classmates tried to persuade Michael to join in a game. They darted past him, shouting, "What are you looking for, Michael? Never seen fog before?"

He ignored them all and gazed intently into the fog. By now he was starting to worry about Mr. Browser. Perhaps he shouldn't have given him the message. Suppose the Brain Sharpeners had lured Mr. Browser into the giant pepperpot and made off with him? Michael looked at the children playing near him. He was just about to risk another walk on the field when a piercing whistle brought all the children to a standstill.

Miss Toms, the assistant principal, was on duty. She had come to the middle of the playground in order to be able to see as many children as possible. Now she was glaring at them as though the children themselves were to blame for the fog.

"No one will move until I say so," she threatened them. "Now, Grades One, Two, and Three, march in."

The smaller children set off for the entrance

door. Miss Toms moved toward the field just as Michael made a half-hearted attempt to disappear into the fog.

"Michael Fairlie!" shouted Miss Toms. "Don't you dare move! One more step, and you can go straight to my room."

Everyone knew that an invitation to visit Miss Tom's room meant nothing but trouble. The assistant principal took a hearty dislike to anyone who disobeyed her. She would set out to make the culprit's life unpleasant for at least a week. So Michael stood still, leaving Mr. Browser to his fate. Gradually Miss Toms worked her way up the grades. Finally the fifth grade was called, and Michael reluctantly joined his friends heading for the door.

"Your shoes are very muddy, Michael!" said Miss Toms as he passed her. "You've been on that field, haven't you? Stand still while I'm talking to you!"

"Yes, Miss Toms."

"Yes? Why, Michael, why?"

This time Michael came up with a more

likely story. "I ran to get my ball, Miss Toms," he said.

Miss Toms gave him one of her sharpest looks. "Where's your ball now?" she demanded. "You must have been digging for it, judging by the amount of mud on those shoes!"

"One of my friends has it," Michael answered.

"Oh well. Move along now. And wipe those shoes well at the door."

"Yes, Miss Toms."

How Michael wanted to tell Miss Toms the truth! Perhaps, for once, she wouldn't seem so sure of herself. More probably she would send him straight to her room for being fresh. He tried to console himself with the thought that one day she might find out the truth from Mr. Browser— if he ever came back!

Michael was the last to enter the classroom, after being delayed by Miss Toms and by the thorough cleaning of his shoes. He found the class making the most of Mr. Browser's absence. Simon Jackson (nicknamed Spiky because of the spike of black hair that was once again standing straight up from the crown of his head) was about to throw a paper airplane. Jason was risking an indoor game of marbles with Jeff Smith on the floor. Anna Cardwell was doing a dance in front of the blackboard. And several of the children were still standing in what Mr. Browser called Gossip Corner.

Steven Simmons was busy preparing his G.I. Joe for an attack on Sarah Mount's Barbie doll. Jennifer Charman and her friend Alison Gilpin, who were both crazy about horses, were fixing saddles on two lifelike models. Bobby Stine

seemed to be working, but a closer look revealed that he was lost in a comic strip about a space adventure.

Michael saw all this as he passed by on the way to his desk. He was tempted to shout "Be quiet!"—because outside on the field a real-life space adventure was going on, and Mr. Browser was caught up in it. But even as that thought entered his mind, he felt a little dizzy. The Brain Sharpeners were keeping in touch with him. This frightened Michael. He sat down at his desk with his head in his hands.

"Whatever is going on here? The oldest children in the school, setting such a bad example for the rest! I suppose I couldn't expect you to come into school and settle down to work on your own! Sit down, all of you!"

The thunderous voice belonged to the principal, Mr. Salt. He crossed the classroom to Mr. Browser's desk and banged his fist down on it.

"Just because Mr. Browser isn't here"—and he looked around sternly to see where Mr. Browser might be—"we don't expect you to behave as though it's a holiday! Take out a book, each of you, and see that you're quiet until he comes!"

The class meekly obeyed. After a minute or two, Mr. Salt decided that he could safely leave them. As he walked across the classroom, he realized that he hadn't seen Mr. Browser that morning.

"Has anyone seen Mr. Browser?" he asked.

To Michael's relief no one answered at first. But just as Mr. Salt set off again, Anna piped up.

"He's at school, Mr. Salt. I saw his car in the lot. And I saw him talking to Michael Fairlie. I was coming down the road by the parking lot at the time."

"Indeed," said Mr. Salt, intrigued. "Michael, was Mr. Browser talking to you? Why didn't you put your hand up? What was he talking about? And where did he go afterwards?"

Michael was confused. Perspiration appeared on his forehead.

"Please, Mr. Salt. He was only talking to me for a minute. He told me to go back to the playground."

"And where did he go?"

"Out on the field, Mr. Salt."

"Why do you suppose he did that, Michael? It seems an odd thing to do."

"Please sir—"

"Well, Michael?"

Michael's head fell forward on the desk.

"Mr. Salt, Michael's fainted," Anna cried.

Mr. Salt hurried to Michael's side. To his surprise, he found that it was true. Michael was unconscious, slumped over his desk.

"Open the window. Give him air," the principal commanded. He quickly loosened Michael's shirt. "You're all right, son," Mr. Salt said, as Michael groaned a little and began to open his eyes. "Haven't you had any breakfast? Perhaps it's the fog that's upset you. I was only asking you about Mr. Browser. I'm not going to punish you—though of course you shouldn't have been in the parking lot. I shall have to ask Mr. Browser about that when I see him."

"I am here, Mr. Salt."

All the class, including Michael, turned toward the doorway where Mr. Browser stood.

"How odd he looks," Anna whispered. "Just like when—"

"Ah, Mr. Browser," said the principal. "We were just trying to find out where you were, and Michael here suddenly became ill. I think he's better now, though. Perhaps you'll take over the class. I have a parent waiting to see me downstairs."

"Of course, Mr. Salt. I'll look after Michael."

"I'm all right," said Michael. He was beginning to feel much better now that Mr. Browser was safely back from his visit to the Brain Sharpeners. As for Mr. Salt, he was so glad to have Mr. Browser back with the class that he didn't bother to ask where he'd been. Anna, however, was still curious. As soon as the principal left, she risked putting a question to Mr. Browser.

"Where have you been, Mr. Browser? Please tell us!"

She was ready for a mild rebuke from Mr. Browser, but she was far from prepared for what happened.

"From now on," said Mr. Browser angrily,

"you will cease to be impertinent, Anna Cardwell. You will settle down and concentrate on your work. Your ignorance is appalling. So is that of the rest of the class. I am going to turn this class into the smartest set of children in this school. Yes, the smartest. And not only in this school, but in the state, in the country, and in the whole world!"

"What a hope!" muttered Spiky Jackson. Half the class burst out laughing.

"Enough!" ordered Mr. Browser. "The time for jokes is past. This morning, just as a beginning, we will learn all our tables to perfection. You'll need to know them for the complicated mathematics we'll be learning in the next few days. Books and pencils ready! Not a second is to be wasted!"

Silently the children opened their books. Michael took the opportunity to look into Mr. Browser's eyes. The change that he saw there told him everything. The Brain Sharpeners had taken full control of Mr. Browser.

3★

More Homework Please!

Mr. Salt, the principal of Chivvy Chase School, was a tall and serious man who wanted—even demanded—everything and everybody in his school to be perfect. It was said that when he walked across the school grounds, each blade of grass stood up straight and the birds all sang in tune. So what he had seen in Mr. Browser's classroom—Spiky Jackson throwing his paper airplane, Anna Cardwell dancing in front of the blackboard—upset him very much.

Mr. Salt was angry with the children for misbehaving. But he was even more angry with Mr. Browser for not being in his classroom at the

29

right time. So when the principal returned to his office, he immediately buzzed his secretary, Miss Copewell.

"Get me the files on the children in Mr. Browser's class, please. Oh, and bring any letters of complaint about the class which we have filed away."

Miss Copewell could tell from the tone of Mr. Salt's voice that he was especially upset. And when she brought the files in she saw that he had taken his glasses off to clean them—another bad sign. He obviously wanted to have a clear look at whatever misfortune was placed in front of him. The principal rubbed hard at the lenses. Miss Copewell put the files down on his desk and left without a word.

"Hm!" Mr. Salt scanned the class list. A likeable lot, he thought. Admittedly, Mr. Browser had no geniuses in his class. When it came to brains, the fifth grade was certainly an average group. He flipped through the cards, picking out a selection of them—including those of students whose parents had for some reason written in to complain about their children's progress.

"Sandra Axford. Slow worker." Yes, thought Mr. Salt. She's interested in nothing but fun and games.

"Peter Brymore. Football crazy." Yes, agreed Mr. Salt. The boy has a crick in his neck from looking out the window when other classes are having games.

"Anna Cardwell. Loves acting. Mischievous. Hates writing and math." Better put in, "likes dancing," too, decided Mr. Salt, recalling Anna's dance that morning.

"Jennifer Charman. Horse crazy." There were several like that.

"Jason Little. Careless. Plays with marbles." True. Mr. Salt had twenty of Jason's marbles in his drawer—and he blamed Mr. Browser for not taking more of them from the boy.

"Simon Jackson. In trouble in and out of school. Does not concentrate." Mr. Salt could only shake his head.

Then there was the Fairlie boy. Michael was quite bright, and he enjoyed writing science fiction stories. Funny how he had fainted. A bit of a dreamer, the principal decided. He gave a little groan and pushed the rest of the files away. The unread ones, he knew, would be pretty much like those he had just read. Still, Mr. Browser should be stricter with them. And why hadn't he been in class on time? Mr. Salt decided to go back to the classroom after assembly and speak to the teacher about it. With any luck he would catch him when the class was noisy. Then he'd have an extra excuse for being critical.

A few minutes after assembly was over, Mr. Salt marched down the corridor to see Mr. Browser. When he reached the classroom door, he was somewhat surprised to hear no sound coming from within. He took a quick look inside and saw that all the children were bent over their books. Mr. Browser was striding up and down the rows with a very severe expression on his face. Mr. Salt turned and crept away. He would find a better time to scold Mr. Browser and the class.

Every half hour or so, the principal returned

to Mr. Browser's room. But each time, much to his surprise, he was greeted by complete silence. All the children—even Spiky Jackson—were giving one hundred percent concentration to their work.

It was uncanny. It was too good to be true. Well, Mr. Browser had evidently sensed the principal's anger and was doing his best to make up for it. I must give him credit where it is due, thought Mr. Salt. And after recess that afternoon he didn't bother to visit the fifth grade any more.

That was a pity. For just before the afternoon ended, Mr. Browser started to relax. In fact, he was beginning to look and act like his old self. Once or twice he went to the window, staring out with a puzzled expression. Michael, too, was able to think of other things besides the Brain Sharpeners. He began feeling better.

"Close your books and put them away," Mr. Browser ordered the class at 3 o'clock. Desks were tidied, and each boy and girl sat up straight, waiting to be dismissed. Mr. Browser stared at a point over the tops of their heads.

"Tomorrow morning, if it's still foggy," he announced, "we'll be going out on the field to measure exactly how far we can see in the fog."

"Wow! I hope it's foggy!" cried Spiky Jackson. The announcement was greeted with enthusiasm by everyone but Michael, who shivered as though he were already out in the fog.

"Class dismissed," said Mr. Browser. Soon there was no one left but Michael, who remained at his desk staring at Mr. Browser.

"Well, Michael?" Mr. Browser asked.

"You're going to take the class out to that pepperpot thing," said Michael. "They've told you to bring us out into the fog, haven't they? They make the fog themselves, Mr. Browser. Did they take you inside that thing? What did they do to you, Mr. Browser? And what do they want to do with us?"

Mr. Browser stood in front of Michael, trying to decide how much to tell him.

"Yes, Michael," he finally answered, "they let me enter their craft. They want us all to go in there tomorrow. They are going to begin a course which will sharpen and extend the

34

brainpower of all the children in the class. That will give me the ability to teach at a very advanced level. They showed me all their equipment. Each child will have a special helmet put on his head. Then brain-developing rays will be shot into their heads for ten minutes. Gradually the length of treatment will increase. Eventually, each brain will be capable of receiving knowledge directly from the Brain Sharpeners, without my help. Michael, there's no telling now how you will end your days. Maybe you'll become a great scientist—or even a leader of the people. The secrets of the universe are going to be made clear to us."

"I wish you'd never thought about the Brain Sharpeners!" declared Michael. "Why are they doing all this for us? What do they want in return?"

Mr. Browser looked down at Michael as though his brain had just returned to earth.

"You'd better go home now, Michael," he said with a frown, "or you'll miss your favorite television program."

Inside the Spacecraft

"It's a foggy day again, Mr. Browser. Are we going out on the field? You promised we could."

Spiky Jackson was always eager to do anything that did not involve sitting at a desk and writing.

"Yes. All right, Simon," replied Mr. Browser. "We'll be going out soon after assembly."

"I think it's silly to go out in the fog," said Anna.

"Don't be a spoilsport," Spiky muttered.

As Mr. Browser called the roll, Michael crept out and stood silently beside him.

"What's the matter, Michael?" Mr. Browser

asked when he had checked off the last name.

"Do you think it's a good idea to go out there again, Mr. Browser? I've been thinking about the Brain Sharpeners. I'm sure they're not up to any good—not for us, anyway!"

Mr. Browser closed the roll book.

"I wouldn't worry, Michael, if I were you. I don't believe the Brain Sharpeners will be back. In fact, I think I must have dreamed the whole thing up!"

"But you didn't, Mr. Browser. I saw them too. The Brain Sharpeners tried to take charge of my brain. You saw how I passed out yesterday—"

"Lack of air, Michael," said Mr. Browser. "No, I don't believe they'll do us any harm."

"There's only one way to stop them from taking us over completely," whispered Michael. "We must try not to think about them. Refuse to concentrate while they're around. Otherwise we'll become their slaves!"

"Nonsense, Michael. Go and sit down!"

"What were you whispering about, Michael?" demanded Spiky, when Michael returned to his seat. "What's the big secret?"

Michael was tempted to tell Spiky. But just as he was about to explain, the bell for assembly rang. Perhaps it was just as well he hadn't said anything, Michael thought, watching Spiky slide down the banister. His friend probably would have laughed at him.

Michael sat through assembly without hearing a word of Mr. Salt's speech. The principal's voice was a meaningless drone as he told a story of somebody's brave deed. Michael's mind was on the Brain Sharpeners. More and more he was coming to believe that it was his duty to discover what plans they had for his class. He had a feeling that they were up to no good.

When the assembly was over, the class went back to the room. Mr. Browser joined them after getting his overcoat.

"Put your coats on," he told them. "We're going out for a while to do a little math. We are going to estimate how far we can see in the fog. We won't be outside for very long."

Nearly everyone greeted this announcement

happily. Like Spiky Jackson, the other children thought anything was better than normal work at their desks. Michael reluctantly joined the end of the line. Mr. Browser led them down the stairs and out through the main entrance. Mr. Salt was standing in the doorway.

"Taking the children outside on a day like this, Mr. Browser?" The principal's look was critical. True, he hadn't been able to find anything wrong in Mr. Browser's class the day before. But he was still suspicious and ready to believe the worst about the fifth grade.

"Only for a little while, Mr. Salt," Mr. Browser replied. "We're doing some practical mathematics. Estimating how far we can see in the fog."

Mr. Salt couldn't say no to this, but he was uneasy. "Jackson, move quietly about the school, or you'll be staying inside."

"Yes, Mr. Salt."

So the principal let them pass. They marched along the front of the school building and down the path which led to the playground.

"There's something hissing!" said Spiky.

"Can't hear anything," Michael replied. But of course he could. He knew the Brain Sharpeners were back. And either they had timed their visit perfectly, or Mr. Browser had timed his little expedition to the field at precisely the right moment.

"There's a wind coming up," said Anna. "The fog's blowing away."

"No it isn't," said Michael. "It's the pepperpot landing."

"He's pepperpotty!" Spiky mocked.

Michael kept calm. "You'll see," was all he said.

By the time Michael stepped on the grass, Mr. Browser and the boys at the front of the line were lost in puffs of fog. As Michael approached the middle of the field, he expected to be met by a shaft of light like the one he'd seen before. But no light appeared. And he heard no sounds from those ahead of him. Maybe the pepperpot wasn't there after all.

After a few more steps, however, Michael

realized why he had heard and seen nothing. The pepperpot revealed in front of him this time was protected by a circle of light. And it looked ten times bigger than the first one he had seen. Mr. Browser was standing at the door, watching the class file up some steps leading inside. Michael was filled with fear as he realized the power of the Brain Sharpeners. Today they had a pepperpot big enough to accommodate the

whole class. Next time they might have one large enough to hold a whole school. Who could tell what the Brain Sharpeners might attempt? If they were unfriendly, they could soon take control of thousands of people and use them to suit their own ends.

"Mr. Browser! This pepperpot is ten times bigger!" Michael called out as he reached the steps. But Mr. Browser ignored him. Michael could tell by the expression on his teacher's face that Mr. Browser was already under the influence of the Brain Sharpeners. Michael stood still.

"Inside, Michael!" Mr. Browser ordered sternly.

Michael thought about running away. But then what? He knew he'd find it hard to persuade people to listen to his story. Besides, he had learned from the stories of old heroes that it is often better to fight your enemies secretly from within their ranks than from the outside. The story of the Greeks and their Trojan horse sprang to mind. In a flash he knew what he had to do. After his first encounter with the Brain Sharpen-

42

ers, Michael had noticed that their power over him lessened as soon as he began thinking of other things. This time, while pretending to obey them, he must try to keep part of his mind otherwise occupied.

As he walked into their brain-sharpening classroom, Michael tried to think about his favorite television program. He saw that each child was being seated in a small, individual alcove. These alcoves were at different levels in the walls of the pepperpot. Everyone was taken to an alcove by a crane which scooped up the children in a seat and hoisted them to the nearest

vacant place. Michael was lifted to an alcove high up. As soon as Mr. Browser had been placed at a large central desk down below, the door of the pepperpot closed.

Each child's head was resting in a kind of half-helmet. Soon the first sharpening got under way. It began with gentle vibrations and rhythmic knockings. Then rays of varying colors darted from the walls and made contact with the helmets. The children sat like hypnotized rabbits waiting to be pounced upon by hungry snakes.

This, thought Michael, is the way brains like Spiky Jackson's will be encouraged to concentrate in the future! Everybody will come to school with the intention of learning. And everybody will have the powers of concentration to do it.

As for Mr. Browser, he was enveloped in an absolute rainbow of rays. Much to his surprise, Michael found the sharpening sensation temptingly pleasant. It would be so easy to give himself up to it and allow his brain to be completely taken over. But Michael was determined to keep

a corner of his mind free. He tried to recall in detail the whole of a children's television play he had seen the night before. He would try to protect just one tiny part of his brain for as long as possible.

Meanwhile, the brain-sharpening machines were hard at work. The class sat patiently, allowing the rays to work their will. Like sheep, thought Michael. He began to count—not to call up sleep but to keep that little section of his mind free.

Nearly ten minutes passed before the vibrations stopped and the rays faded away. Perhaps the Brain Sharpeners were afraid that brittle brains like those of Spiky Jackson and Jason Little would not be able to take too much sharpening at one time. Mr. Browser stood up, and the crane returned all the children to the floor. Then the door opened and Mr. Browser walked out. He had no trouble controlling the children now. They all followed him, exactly in step, with serious expressions on their faces. Mr. Browser didn't even bother to count them— which turned out to be a mistake.

As the door of the pepperpot closed, Michael hid behind a square, boxlike shape on the right-hand side of the floor. The hissing noise began again. As the pepperpot prepared to take off, a powerful sound could be heard above the hissing. There was a pause, and then a sound in reply from the pepperpot. Seconds later, the machine translated the message and spoke in English to Michael.

"Why are you still here, boy? You have disobeyed your master. The Brain Sharpeners are displeased."

Michael swiftly realized that a good offense was the best form of defense. "I don't believe in Brain Sharpeners," he said, "and I won't until I see one!"

There came a jumble of noise as the pepperpot translated the message and received a reply. The answer was clearly an order. The pepperpot began to rise. The Brain Sharpeners had accepted his challenge. Michael was on his way to outer space.

5 ★

Instant Learning

While Michael was being whirled away in the giant pepperpot, his classmates were marching in perfect formation back into school. Mr. Browser walked behind them. Nobody spoke and nobody stepped out of line, which was not usually the case with this class.

They trooped into school, along the corridor and up the stairs, and entered their classroom without a word from Mr. Browser. Once in the classroom, books were taken out and pencils made ready immediately. As soon as Mr. Browser began to talk, everyone was prepared to write down his words of wisdom. A dream class, many teachers would have said.

First Mr. Browser explained the importance of them doing their homework each night. "To start with, three hours will be enough," he informed them.

"May we do more if we wish?" asked Spiky Jackson.

Coming from Spiky, this would normally have brought a gust of laughter from the whole class. The thought of Spiky doing any homework at all would have been hard enough to believe. But now nobody made any comment. Nobody even smiled.

"I don't wish to stop anyone from doing more," said Mr. Browser. "Do as much as you like, Simon. I am pleased to hear that you want to make a good start."

"So do I," called out Anna.

"Let us continue with some math. Since our batteries are freshly charged, so to speak, I will explain the theory of Pythagoras to you. For homework you can work some examples."

Mr. Browser began drawing earnestly on the blackboard. The class watched him in absolute silence. At that moment Mr. Salt entered. He had been worried about the children's visit to the foggy field and had secretly watched their return. He noticed that the fog had thinned out and almost vanished by the time the last child entered the school. Mr. Salt had a sneaky suspicion that the students had been wasting their time. He decided to check up on Mr. Browser.

Mr. Salt stood still when he saw how intently the children were watching their teacher's drawing. And when he saw the subject of Mr.

Browser's work, he decided to retreat. But Mr. Browser wouldn't let him.

"Good morning, Mr. Salt. We are just learning about Pythagoras and his theory," he said, turning like a robot toward the principal. "The sum of the squares—"

"Yes, yes," said the principal hastily. "I used to teach Pythagoras to my brightest pupils when I was teaching. But do you think this class is ready for it? I thought some of them were still rather weak at their tables!"

In truth, Mr. Salt couldn't remember much about the theory himself.

"We will all have mastered this by tomorrow," announced Mr. Browser proudly. "Then I'll go on to more advanced work. Logarithms, for example."

"Logarithms," repeated the principal. He vaguely recalled that he had been taught about them in junior high school at the age of about thirteen, not in grammar school at the age of ten. He changed the subject.

"I hope you found your expedition into the

fog worthwhile," he said to the class.

Before anyone could reply, Mr. Browser answered for them. "We achieved what we set out to do," he assured the principal. "It was very worthwhile."

"And just in time, too," observed Mr. Salt. "The fog seems to have cleared up completely."

As he looked toward the window, he caught sight of Michael's empty place at the side of the room.

"One missing, I see. Is there someone absent?

No, I remember. Michael Fairlie sits there. He was here first thing this morning. Where is he now, Mr. Browser?"

The principal believed that he had finally found something wrong in the class. Pleased with himself, he awaited an answer. Knowing Michael, he thought that perhaps the boy had stayed outside and Mr. Browser hadn't noticed. Mr. Browser looked confused for a second. Then Spiky Jackson piped up.

"I think Michael stayed behind with the Br—" he began. But the words died on his lips and his mouth hung open as if he had lockjaw.

Mr. Browser's confusion changed to anger. "I'll certainly look into it, Mr. Salt," he said. "I think he must have slipped out into the coat-room. And now, please, we must waste no more time. We have much to do today. Excuse me please, Mr. Salt. The sum of the squares—"

All eyes were directed to the blackboard. Mr. Salt's presence was at once forgotten. He stood there for a few seconds, feeling rather a nuisance. It was a feeling he didn't much like.

"Carry on, Mr. Browser," the principal said, leaving the room. On his way back to his office, he looked into the coatroom, but Michael wasn't there.

"There's something odd about Mr. Browser's class, Miss Copewell," the principal told his secretary moments later. "They're all working hard in there doing math which ought to be miles beyond them. Yet they seem to be enjoying it."

"You should be pleased about that," said Miss Copewell, who always looked on the bright side of things. "Perhaps it's the modern methods Mr. Browser uses."

The principal gave her a sharp look and started studying some forms.

"Well, he's lost that Michael Fairlie," he muttered. "I must go back in a while and make sure that he's returned."

When he checked Mr. Browser's class half an hour later, Mr. Salt saw at once that Michael's place was still vacant. The class was hard at work copying something from the blackboard. Mr.

Browser crossed to the door to meet him.

"Michael has just gone to the library, Mr. Salt," he said before the principal could speak.

"So he's come back," said Mr. Salt. "What was he up to?"

"Oh, too enthusiastic about experimenting in the fog," Mr. Browser explained. "He was far away when we came in. Lost himself for a while."

"Oh," said Mr. Salt. "I see."

"Perhaps you'd like to inspect our work," Mr. Browser went on. "We have a considerable amount of math to cover, but I think that with effort we shall be up to high school math by the end of the school year."

"I beg your pardon. Do you mean geometry and trigonometry which are for children of fifteen or sixteen, Mr. Browser?"

"Yes, Mr. Salt, and I mean it. And by the way, have we any copies of Shakespeare in the school? I would like to study *Hamlet* with the class next term, if possible."

"I thought you were reading *The Wind in the*

55

Willows," said Mr. Salt weakly.

"That's kids' stuff, Mr. Salt!" called out Spiky Jackson. "Buy us some Shakespeare, Mr. Salt. Give us something to think about."

Mr. Salt looked at Spiky Jackson as though he had never seen the boy before.

"We'll see about it, Simon," he muttered, making a quick exit and heading for his office.

"Miss Copewell," he gasped, when his secretary came in with a cup of tea. "Simon Jackson wants to study Shakespeare. He could be going for his college entrance exams this summer. This summer, Linda! Think of it! At eleven years old. Simon Jackson, of all people!"

"Spiky Jackson," said Miss Copewell, who could tell that Mr. Salt was under stress because he'd called her Linda. "Have your tea, Mr. Salt. It's nice and hot. Perhaps you'd like me to get you an aspirin to take with it?"

"Yes, please!" begged the principal. He gulped down a mouthful of too-hot tea to try to calm his nerves.

6★

Michael's Close Encounter

As the pepperpot zoomed into space, Michael was puzzled. He had expected to have trouble with weightlessness, but he found that he could walk about as though he were still on the ground. Maybe we're just circling the world, he thought.

"Where are we?" he asked. "Aren't we out in space yet?"

The translating machine set to work. Soon an answer came back.

"We are a hundred thousand miles beyond your moon. We are on course toward our Intermediate Space Station. There you will meet

one of our Outer Space Commanders. He's a most important Brain Sharpener."

"Thank you," said Michael. "Where is the home of the Brain Sharpeners?"

There was a pause while the translating machine did its work, and the answering system considered whether the question was one that could safely be answered.

"Our world is not far away," the machine replied at last. "We live on a planet in a nearby galaxy. It has a climate similar to yours. That is why we are interested in Earth. We have discovered several other planets near our own. We want to develop them, and we need to recruit more citizens to colonize them. Life on your world has not developed as fast as on ours, and of course our brains are much superior. We think your people will be pleased to have their brains sharpened by us and to start a new life in one of our colonies—especially when they find out what we have achieved with your Mr. Browser and his class."

Big heads! thought Michael. Then, just in case the Brain Sharpeners were reading his thoughts, he said aloud, "Thank you very much for the information!"

The flight continued for another hour.

"We are preparing to land," the machine finally announced. There followed the usual hissing sound, and the pepperpot gently sank down. The door opened.

"You may step out," said the machine, and Michael obeyed. He saw that the pepperpot had flown onto a huge enclosed platform. Above

him a transparent roof was closing. It had opened up to allow their entry.

"Stand still!" a voice ordered. "You will be taken to the Commander."

Michael looked around for someone to lead him, but instead the floor beneath him began to move. He looked down, fascinated, as his section of the floor carried him to the door of one of the many rooms at the back of the platform. The door slid open, and Michael's piece of floor deposited him at the entrance.

"Walk in," said a voice.

Sitting behind a desk was a tall, humanlike person with long arms and a large but handsome head. The alien looked at him with a gaze so sharp that Michael felt as if he were staring into the sun.

"Welcome," said the figure. "You wished to see a Brain Sharpener. Now you are looking at one. Is there anything more you wish to know?"

"Yes, please," said Michael, avoiding that penetrating gaze. "Why are you interfering with my world—and why particularly with my class?"

"I thought the machine had told you that," remarked the Brain Sharpener.

"I'd like to confirm it," said Michael. "Machines can make mistakes."

"Not ours," said the Brain Sharpener. "However, I will answer your question. When we first discovered your world, we could not believe how backward its people were. Dangerous, too. If they go on advancing scientifically, they may destroy themselves and lay waste to the whole planet. We considered two ways of preventing that. One was to destroy your planet. But we would only do that if we were threatened ourselves. The other way was to improve your brains so that you would be fit to survive, as well as to help us develop our other planets. Do you understand this?"

Too well, thought Michael. It's slavery for most of us. Then he decided he'd better try to control his critical thoughts, in case the Brain Sharpeners were tuning in to them.

"Why did you choose my class?" he asked, to change the subject.

"Your teacher, Mr. Browser, spoke words that put him in direct contact with us for a short while. No one else ever mentioned Brain Sharpeners while we were listening in to the planet Earth. We realized afterwards that the words had only been spoken by chance. But as we were already thinking about contacting Earth, why not your class? Your brains certainly could do with some sharpening, I'm sure you will agree."

"And you have already begun sharpening their brains?"

"Of course. And from reports already received, the work is going very well."

"What will happen to them when you've sharpened their brains enough?"

The Commander's expression remained earnest. He never relaxed his concentration.

"We shall consider them for transfer to our fifth newly discovered planet, which we are trying to develop."

"But they are only children," said Michael.

"Precisely. We need children. By the time they arrive at their destination they will be just the right age for settling down."

"An excellent idea," said Michael, hoping that the Brain Sharpener would not be able to read his secret thoughts—which were full of fear.

What an awful prospect! His friends in school were already busy preparing themselves to be kidnapped! At all costs he must return and warn them—if they would listen. If not, he would have to speak to the principal or contact their parents. Meanwhile he must try to keep his own mind out of the Brain Sharpeners' clutches.

"As for you," the Commander continued, "I

have satisfied your wish to meet a Brain Sharpener. If you were to stay here and take a concentrated course, you could travel on to Planet Five before the others. By the time they arrived, you would already hold an important position."

"Thank you very much," said Michael, trembling at the idea. "It's a great compliment. But don't you think that if I stayed here people on Earth would wonder what had happened to

me? There'd be an awful fuss in the newspapers. Perhaps you don't know what newspapers on Earth are like. When I came back—if I ever did—there'd be reporters around me like flies around honey. And if I came back smarter than before, people would be suspicious. At the moment, Mr. Browser is getting all the credit. No one suspects the presence of an outside power. I think the best thing would be to send me back quickly, just the same as when I left. If I work hard, I'm sure Mr. Browser will help me catch up with the rest. You don't want anything to go wrong until you're sure our brains can be sharpened enough for your purposes."

"Good sense," observed the Commander. "Once we have sharpened your brain, you should have a great future on Planet Five. I will arrange to have you transferred back to Earth. You will be deposited on your school field as soon as it gets dark."

Michael stepped outside and onto the moving floor again. This time it guided him to a very small spacecraft, barely large enough to hold one small person. The door closed behind him as soon as he entered. Then the transparent roof above the platform opened up. The tiny craft ascended through the gap and rocketed to Earth.

Several sightings of a UFO were reported that evening. But nobody saw Michael step onto the school field just after dark. As soon as he had done so, the little spacecraft began disintegrating. Within two minutes there was nothing but a small burnt mark on the grass to show that it had ever existed.

Michael ran across the field and into the school. Mr. Browser was still in the classroom. He was putting books into his briefcase and preparing to leave.

"Michael! You're back! You've missed a whole day's work! You'll have to make up for it tomorrow!"

"Yes, Mr. Browser." Michael was disappointed. In the old days, before the Brain Sharpeners started interfering, Mr. Browser would have wanted to know whether Michael was all right and would have told him to hurry home to his parents. Now all he cared about was the missing of a day's work!

Michael rushed home, very depressed. His prospects for rescuing his classmates from their outer-space fate seemed far from rosy. He certainly could expect no help from Mr. Browser.

Mr. Browser was already beginning to act just like a Brain Sharpener!

7★

An Unhappy Homecoming

As soon as Michael entered the school playground the next morning, he could see how much the Brain Sharpeners had changed his classmates in just one day.

Spiky Jackson, Anna Cardwell, and Jason Little were already there. But they were not fooling around in the playground as they'd always done before. Instead, they were waiting at the school door, anxious to be first inside.

"What's the rush, Spiky? Are they giving ice cream away this morning?" Michael asked.

"No, they're not," replied Spiky, as though Michael had asked a serious question. Anna and some of the others frowned at Michael. He saw that they were all carrying notebooks.

"What went on yesterday? What are the notebooks for?"

At first no one answered him.

"Haven't you done any homework?" Anna finally asked.

"Homework? Of course not. There'll be plenty of time for that in junior high school."

"I did four hours last night," said Spiky Jackson, looking highly pleased about it.

"Four hours? You, Spiky? Impossible! You haven't gone bananas, have you?"

Spiky flipped through his notebook. The pages were filled with neat writing. Michael could hardly believe it was Spiky's.

"You'll have to work hard to catch up with us, Michael," said Spiky.

"I won't have much time to catch up today—what with a television program this morning and games this afternoon," observed Michael. "Are we playing football?"

"There won't be any playtime this afternoon,"

put in Anna. "We've agreed to cancel our games from now on. Mr. Browser says we need all the time available in order to achieve what he's set out to do this term."

"You're joking," Michael protested weakly. But there wasn't a sign of mischief in Anna's expression.

"TV has been cut out too," Spiky informed him. "Waste of time, Mr. Browser says. He wants us to concentrate on math and science this term. If we do enough homework, he thinks we'll be up to high school level by Easter."

The rest of the children were now crowding around the door. They were all as excited as Spiky and Anna. Michael's heart sank. The Mr. Browser he knew would never have cancelled games on a fine day or cut out the weekly television program.

"You're being tricked!" he shouted to them all. "You and Mr. Browser are being used by the Brain Sharpeners! If they think they can make you sharp enough, they'll take you off to Planet Five, and you'll never come back. You'll be kidnapped!"

The other members of the class stared at Michael as though he himself were something from outer space. Then they turned away from him as a bell sounded inside the school. A few seconds later, Miss Toms opened the door.

"Grade Five—you all seem anxious to go inside today," she remarked. She usually had to round up Spiky Jackson—and sometimes Michael—from the far end of the playground.

"We've some work to hand in to Mr. Browser," Spiky explained.

"Indeed," said Miss Toms, giving him an odd look. "Well, if that's so, I'd better let you in first. Here—careful! Don't knock me over!"

Michael followed the eager students, who were up the hallway and stairs and into the classroom in a flash.

"Good morning, class," said Mr. Browser. They were all sitting in their seats waiting for him as he sat down at his desk like a robot. "I trust you have completed all the suggested homework?"

The class, with the exception of Michael, answered together with enthusiasm.

"Then I trust we can look forward to another day of concentrated learning," Mr. Browser went on. "I'll call the roll first."

When he came to Michael's name he stopped uneasily.

"Michael," he asked, "have you done any homework?"

"No, Mr. Browser. I was away yesterday."

"I remember," said Mr. Browser, frowning. "You will have to work extra hard today in order to catch up with the rest of the class. Perhaps you can do an hour or two of extra homework tonight."

"Yes, Mr. Browser."

An hour or two of extra homework! Mr. Browser had been turned into a slave driver. Michael decided to try and play along with him and the rest of the class. But it was sad to see Mr. Browser so changed by the Brain Sharpeners. It would be no use trying to persuade him that he and his class were in grave danger. Michael would have to find another way of fighting the Brain Sharpeners.

Several days passed in concentrated study at school followed by hours of homework each night. When the weekend came, the whole class, with the exception of Michael, looked sad at the prospect of a break in the learning routine. Mr. Browser, too, was worried about this. He tried to make up for it by giving out enough homework to keep the class busy all Saturday and Sunday.

The principal was taking an increasing interest

in the class. His opinion of Mr. Browser was rising steadily. At first he had been suspicious and disbelieving. Once he saw the great progress Mr. Browser had made, however, he was more than happy to bask in some of the glory.

Michael was the only fly in the educational ointment. He was completely out of his depth in all subjects. It was clear that he wasn't doing a tenth of the amount of homework being done by the others.

"Michael," Mr. Salt warned, "if you can't keep up with the rest, I'll have to transfer you. You're the only one who isn't taking advantage of the excellent teaching Mr. Browser is providing."

"I'm the only one who's not being brain-washed," answered Michael.

"Sit down, and don't be so fresh," the principal ordered.

On Monday morning Michael resolved to foil the Brain Sharpeners. Only the principal could save the class, he reasoned, by having Mr. Browser removed from the school. If the class had no more direct contact with the Brain

Sharpeners and their machines, then perhaps the effects would die away and Michael would win back his friends. As soon as he got to school that morning, Michael knocked on Mr. Salt's door. The principal frowned when he saw him.

"Well, Michael," Mr. Salt greeted him. "I trust that you are making more of an effort to please Mr. Browser."

"I've come to see you about Mr. Browser and our class," said Michael. "It's very important. If something isn't done soon, it'll be too late to save them."

"Save them? From what?"

"From the Brain Sharpeners. Mr. Browser is in touch with them, sir. They come from another galaxy. They're trying to sharpen up our brains so they can send us to a planet they want to populate. Unless we can show that our brains can't be developed as much as the Brain Sharpeners require, one day we'll vanish, Mr. Salt, and we'll never come back. We'll be kidnapped by the Brain Sharpeners, Mr. Salt, I'm warning you!"

Michael paused for breath. Mr. Salt sat back in his chair and stared at him. He didn't take kindly to anyone in his school warning him about anything.

"That's quite a speech, Michael," he said at last.

"It's all true, sir."

"Do you really expect me to believe it? I happen to be highly pleased with your class, and with Mr. Browser. You are the only one who gives me cause for concern, Michael. Even if your story were true, I would do all I could to encourage any power that could turn your class into such an excellent group of students. The way they're going, they'll all bring honor to the school. I can just imagine the surprise of the junior high principal when he discovers the superior work of the Chivvy Chase children coming up to him. They'll be far beyond the children from any other school. I am proud of them, Michael. No, my boy, it is not the rest of the children for whom I fear. I fear for you. I would advise you to return to your classroom and buckle down to work, my boy. That's all!"

"You're worse than the Brain Sharpeners!" burst out Michael. But the principal was already shuffling papers. Michael knew he was once again beaten. The Brain Sharpeners were winning. As he left Mr. Salt's room, he realized that he should not have expected any different reaction from a man as proud of his school as Mr. Salt.

All hope seemed lost until he passed Miss Copewell's door and heard voices from within.

"I'd like to have a word with Mr. Salt," a man was saying earnestly. "I don't know what's the matter with my Simon lately. He's behaving in a most curious manner."

"I'm sorry to hear it," said Miss Copewell in her sympathetic voice. "What seems to be the trouble?"

"He's spending all his time working," said Mr. Jackson. "We can't stop him. No time for anything else at all. It's fishy. He's not in trouble any more, it's true, but his behavior isn't normal."

"They do go through funny stages," Miss Copewell informed the worried father. "However, if Mr. Salt is free, I'm sure he'll be pleased to see you."

As Michael stood listening just beyond the office door, a ray of hope warmed him. This was Spiky Jackson's father. He had come to the school because he couldn't understand why his son had suddenly become a bookworm. Maybe other parents would be suspicious, too!

As Michael walked back to class, Mr. Salt

kindly agreed to see Mr. Jackson. But first he gave Miss Copewell some instructions. "Please check in the file and see if there's anything odd about Michael Fairlie and his family," he requested. "Have you noticed anything yourself lately?"

"I can't say I have, Mr. Salt."

"The boy's been in here telling me the most ridiculous story. Behaving like a lunatic. Maybe he's been seeing too many science fiction films, but I would like you to check. And now please send in Mr. Jackson. There's no pleasing some parents. Why, his son has just begun to work hard for the first time. I won't let Mr. Jackson waste much of my time, I can assure you."

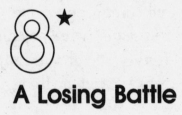

A Losing Battle

The days passed, and the gap between Michael's knowledge and that of the rest of the class continued to increase. Because he wasn't under the influence of the Brain Sharpeners, Michael didn't stand much chance of keeping up. Mr. Browser soon decided that Michael was a lost cause. He allowed him to sit in a corner reading books and even comics while the other children were having their brains further and further extended.

"I'll just have to do something about you, Michael," he occasionally told his one unresponsive pupil. "I can't understand why you don't make any progress. I'll have to find out when next we . . ."

He didn't finish the sentence, but Michael figured that Mr. Browser was expecting to see the Brain Sharpeners again. The teacher seemed to be spending quite a bit of time looking out the window. And Michael was pretty sure he knew why.

"Hoping for some fog, Mr. Browser?" he asked. Mr. Browser frowned and turned away from the window.

Mr. Salt was becoming increasingly proud of the fifth grade. He was overheard telling Mr. Browser that he would bring the district superintendent in to show him how smart the children of Chivvy Chase School had become since he'd been principal.

Not everything, however, was rosy in Mr. Salt's life. First Mr. Jackson had complained about his son's changed outlook on life. Then Mrs. Cardwell came in to protest about the amount of homework Anna was doing.

"But I am assured by Mr. Browser that all the

children love doing their homework," said Mr. Salt. "They keep asking for more."

"So does Anna," agreed her mother. "But it doesn't seem natural. She never has time to help with the housework. And she never listens to her stereo. She hardly seems human any more, Mr. Salt."

"You should be proud of your daughter," the principal insisted. "She'll be a credit to you later on."

"She's not my daughter any more," declared Mrs. Cardwell. "Never laughs or even smiles lately."

Parents are never satisfied, thought Mr. Salt—and he told Mrs. Cardwell so, just as he had told Mr. Jackson. Other parents came up to complain, too. The principal became more and more irritable with them. They should be praising the school not criticizing it, he thought. He had always wanted to have the best school in the country. Now these ignorant parents seemed to be standing in his way.

"Go home and be thankful that you have such smart children," he told them. And Mr. Salt was such an important man to them that most of the parents followed his orders, just as their children had to do.

After about two weeks, Michael was pleased to note that Mr. Browser was not quite as intense as usual. Instead of allowing those who wanted to stay in at recess to remain in the classroom and continue working, he ordered everyone out to the playground.

While the rest of the class reluctantly went outside and hung around the door just waiting to return to work, Michael crept back to the classroom and peeked through the window.

Inside, Mr. Browser was pacing up and down, wiping his forehead with a handkerchief. He sat down at his desk for a while with his head in his hands. Then he stood up again and continued to march up and down. Something was worrying Mr. Browser, but clearly he himself couldn't quite grasp what it was. Michael figured that the Brain Sharpeners' influence must be weakening. Unless Mr. Browser's brain got recharged soon, he would gradually return to normal.

At first Michael was pleased by this thought. But then he thought of the danger that could go with it. The Brain Sharpeners would do all they could to keep Mr. Browser under their influence. No doubt they would be returning on the next foggy day. In fact, Michael thought they might be so satisfied with the class's progress that they would start the children on their journey to Planet Five right away!

And only I can stop them, thought Michael. He recalled the little Dutch boy who had tried to stop the sea from breaking through a dyke, and he felt just as small and helpless. Beads of perspiration appeared on his forehead as he realized that the lives of all his friends on Earth could depend on him alone. He looked up anxiously for signs of fog in the sky, but it was a clear day. Mr. Browser was again at the window, gazing up. How he needed those Brain Sharpeners again!

The day was so still and clear that there might very easily be some mist and fog the next morning. Michael knew he might have less than twenty-four hours in which to save the class. He went down to the playground and watched his friends as they hung around the school door, hungry to be back inside again. There was no point trying to warn them. They were so much under Mr. Browser's influence that they wouldn't even listen to any hint of danger. All he could do, Michael decided, was to try and warn their parents.

He spent the rest of the day obtaining the home addresses of as many of his classmates as possible.

"I may be moving out of town soon, and I'd like to be able to write to you," was his excuse. To his relief, it worked in each case. The poor little mental robots gave him their addresses without any question. Then Michael had only to endure the rest of the school day reading comics and listening to Mr. Browser's voice drone on as he gave out notes like a professor.

In the afternoon Mr. Salt came into the room to check on the class's progress. To tell the truth, though, the lesson was well beyond the mathematical capabilities of Mr. Salt. As far as the principal could tell, it had something to do with finding the optimum stress on the arch of a bridge. As Mr. Salt's attention wandered from the lesson at hand, he caught sight of Michael reading in the corner.

"I'm going to have to remove you from this class, Fairlie," he threatened. "You just aren't keeping up with the rest. I can't have Mr.

Browser's time wasted. I'll have to see about transferring you tomorrow."

Michael was afraid that if he lost all touch with the class, he'd also lose any chance of foiling the Brain Sharpeners.

"Please let me stay, Mr. Salt!" he pleaded. But the principal only muttered something vague and walked away.

At last the bell rang, signaling the end of the day. The students stuffed their homework books into their bags and headed for home—and more work. Michael hurried off too, but he didn't go straight home. He had decided to visit the parents of some of his classmates. First he went to talk to Anna Cardwell's mother. He had seen Mrs. Cardwell in the office at school, and she was friendly with his own parents, so he hoped she would listen sympathetically.

"Hello, Michael. Anna's not home yet," said Mrs. Cardwell.

"It's not Anna I'm here to see, Mrs. Cardwell. It's you. Have you noticed that Anna has been behaving oddly lately?"

"She's been working very hard," admitted Mrs. Cardwell.

"Well, I know why she's like that."

"Do you?" Mrs. Cardwell said sharply. She did not seem as sympathetic as Michael had hoped.

"Yes," Michael went on. "Anna is in the power of some beings from another world. They're called Brain Sharpeners. If we don't stop them, they'll take Anna and all the rest away to another planet. We'll never see them again!"

Mrs. Cardwell took a step back and looked at Michael as though he were an unwanted salesman. "Oh yes? And why did these Brain Sharpeners happen to tell you all this, Michael? Won't they take you as well?"

"No, because I've defied them," Michael explained. "I know what they're up to, and I won't let them control me."

Mrs. Cardwell started laughing.

"Pardon me, Michael, but I can't see that your brain is so much better than Anna's."

"It isn't, Mrs. Cardwell. I just won't let it be sharpened!"

"Sharpened! That's a good joke! Really, Michael, I can't afford to waste any more time. And here's Anna. She'll want a glass of milk while she settles down to her homework. Might I suggest that you run along and do the same?"

"He doesn't do any homework," said Anna with contempt.

"Perhaps he's jealous of those who do," her mother suggested. "Good-bye, Michael."

Michael walked down the garden path with tears in his eyes. Another victory for the Brain Sharpeners! He decided to try Spiky Jackson's house next.

"Excuse me, Mrs. Jackson!"

"Oh hello, Michael. Simon is doing his homework. I hope you don't want him to come out to play. He hasn't any time to spare for that."

"No, Mrs. Jackson. I'm here to tell you the truth about Spi—, I mean Simon. It's not natural that he's working so hard, is it?"

Michael was echoing the words he had heard Mr. Jackson speak to Mr. Salt, but the expected response did not come from her.

"Natural or not, it's doing him no harm. One of these days he'll be a doctor, or a lawyer, or even a politician. We never used to expect anything of him. That's all changed now, though. I want him to make the most of himself. I'd advise you to go home and do some work yourself, Michael Fairlie. According to Simon, you're the class dunce these days!"

"But I heard Mr. Jackson say he was worried

about Simon. I came to warn you about the Brain Sharpeners."

"Brain Sharpeners? You could do with a bit of brain-sharpening yourself, my boy. Mr. Jackson isn't worried any more, Michael. Mr. Salt and I have persuaded him to be sensible. Now he wants Simon to work hard, just as I do. Good-bye, Michael!"

The wretched Spiky Jackson must have heard their voices. But he couldn't even spare the time to get up from his books and come say hello. After that defeat, Michael went sadly on his way. Although the idea of Spiky Jackson as a doctor or a lawyer could have been laughable, the knowledge that the Jacksons were deceiving themselves made Michael despair. Long before Spiky could ever become a doctor, the Brain Sharpeners would have whisked him away to another planet. How could he convince these fond parents that it was better to have normal, free children than smart ones controlled by the Brain Sharpeners?

Michael visited the parents of a few more of his classmates. They all greeted his message with blank looks and outright disbelief. Some laughed, thinking he was joking. One or two called their children away from their homework to ask them what Michael was talking about.

Those clever robot students—formerly Michael's friends—stared at him, said they were sorry, and claimed that *he* had been acting strangely lately. Then they asked if they could please go back to their work—or Mr. Browser would be angry with them. Then the fond parents, proud of their children's new desire to work, grew impatient with Michael and told him to go, closing their doors in his face.

At last Michael accepted the hard truth. The parents would give him no help. They were just as deluded as their children. He even wondered whether the Brain Sharpeners had gotten to them too.

If he was ever going to defeat the Brain Sharpeners, it was clear he would have to do so on his own.

At last Michael set off for home, admitting defeat. As he walked, he saw a low mist forming at the end of the road. The moon was already hidden. He shivered as he realized that the Brain Sharpeners might be coming to collect their victims in the morning.

Michael's Master Plan

Michael woke up early the next morning. Jumping out of bed, he hurried to the window and drew back the curtains.

"Oh, no!" he said. The trees in his own backyard loomed out of the mist, but the houses beyond were hidden. It was a perfect morning for another visit from the Brain Sharpeners. If they were capable of creating the fog themselves, they had done quite a job this time.

"I haven't see a fog this thick in years," declared Michael's mother. "And certainly not at this time of year."

As Michael dressed, he tried to prepare

himself for his coming battle of wits with the
Brain Sharpeners. If only his own brain could be
sharpened—without their help, of course! He
was thinking hard as he ate his cereal, thinking
hard as he drank his juice, thinking hard as he
brushed his teeth. His mother had never seen
him so thoughtful.

"Are you having a test today, Michael?" she
asked, as he absent-mindedly put on his coat,
pushing the buttons into the wrong holes.

"No, Mother."

"Do you feel okay?"

"Yes, Mother."

"Well, be careful on the road in this fog," she said worriedly. "Don't go walking along in a dream and hit your head on a lamppost. I really don't know what's come over you lately!"

Michael set off down the road, still trying to think. Thinking is seldom unrewarded if we keep at it long enough. And by the time he'd reached the school gate, a plan had formed in Michael's mind. Putting it into operation would be risky, but it seemed the only way to fight the Brain Sharpeners.

Michael walked down the path toward the school. To his relief, he heard no sounds from the playground. He was very early, so there was a good chance that no one would see him. He rounded the school building and made for the playground. No one was there. Crossing it quickly, he ran out into the fog. He trotted across the football field. Then, with his heart throbbing and his throat dry, he headed for the fence on the far side of the field. As soon as it loomed up out of the fog, he stopped running. He walked alongside it to a gate which was not used by the children, but was for the janitor and gardener.

He tried the gate, and it opened. Michael was relieved, for it would have been difficult to climb over. He went through to the road outside. A few yards away stood a telephone booth. He had known it was there, but he wanted to make sure it wasn't out of order. The booth would play an important part in his plan.

After checking out the phone, Michael returned to the school grounds. In the corner of the field stood an old shed used by the gardener. Michael hid behind it, listening to the distant sound of the children who were now entering the playground in increasing numbers. The bell rang, and then there was silence. He was tempted to rush across the field and join his friends as they went into the school. Instead, he forced himself to stay and wait for the Brain Sharpeners to arrive.

Minute by minute, the fog thickened. Hiding

behind the shed was soon unnecessary. It was most unlikely that the gardener would turn up for work on such a morning. Michael came out from behind the shed and edged along the fence in order to be near the telephone booth. If the Brain Sharpeners did come, he would have a great deal to do in a very short time. He was considering what excuse he would use for being late to school if they didn't come. Then, from somewhere up above, there came that familiar whirring sound.

The Brain Sharpeners were coming! He waited for a second to be sure. Then he ran through the gate and down the road to the telephone booth, moving faster than he had ever moved in his life. To his relief, the booth was empty. He pulled open the heavy door, lifted the receiver, and dialed 911.

"Police!" he panted into the phone. "There's a body in the middle of the field at Chivvy Chase School. Yes, the school on Chase Road. I was just passing by, and I could see it from the pavement. Please come quickly!"

Without giving any further information, Michael hung up and burst out of the booth. He hoped that the police would come even if they suspected it might be a hoax. Back onto the grounds he ran, along the edge of the field and toward the school. The whirring sound was louder now. Most people would probably have mistaken the noise for that of a plane, or even a gust of wind. But Michael knew better.

He ran across the playground and panted his way into school. His first stop was not his classroom but the principal's office. There he found Miss Copewell. She was busy churning out mimeographed sheets. Michael knocked because he knew that if he didn't there would be a delay while he was scolded for not knocking and treated to a lecture on manners. Miss Copewell's machine stopped.

"Well, Michael?"

"Please, Miss Copewell, Mr. Browser would like the keys to his room. The catch isn't working properly, and he wants to keep the door closed."

"Oh, Michael," said Miss Copewell, handing

him the keys. "The trouble with these doors is that they're not childproof!"

Michael hurried down the hallway, up the stairs, and into the classroom. The children had their heads down as they copied some notes. Mr. Browser was sitting at his desk.

"Sorry I'm late, Mr. Browser," said Michael. "I've just come from the doctor's."

Mr. Browser looked at him with little interest. The teacher's attention was focused on the windows. Michael recognized the symptoms. Mr. Browser was becoming restless. In a moment or two he would ask the class to stand. Then he would lead them out to the pepperpot! It musn't happen again, Michael thought.

"Please, Mr. Browser," he said loudly. "I want to catch up with the rest of the class. May I have a new book from the storeroom? My old one is full. If I'm going to do four hours of homework a night, I'll need a new one badly!"

Mr. Browser stared at him and saw only keenness and a desire to learn on Michael's face. The Brain Sharpeners must be working on him, the teacher thought, mentally welcoming Michael back like a lost sheep that has been found. There might be just enough time to give him a book before the Brain Sharpeners arrived.

"Good, Michael," he said. "Come with me at once. We shall be going out on the field any moment now."

"Of course, Mr. Browser," said Michael.

Mr. Browser hurried across to the storeroom, and Michael followed him. In went Mr. Browser. Quickly Michael closed the door behind his

teacher and turned the storeroom key in the lock. He slipped that key into his jeans pocket alongside the key to the classroom. Then he ran to the door. "Let me out!" shouted Mr. Browser. "This is no time for joking, Michael. I must get out. We have to go to the field. Open the door! Somebody let me out!"

Mr. Browser began to bang on the inside of the door. But by the time some heads had come up from their books, Michael was at the classroom door. He opened it, stepped into the corridor, and locked the door on the class.

Triumphant, he leaned back against the wall to regain his breath. Just then the principal came down the hall. He was on his way to tell Mr. Browser that the district supervisor was coming to the school to check on the fifth grade's marvelous progress.

"What's the matter, Michael?" Mr. Salt asked irritably. He had suddenly remembered his threat to have Michael transferred to another class. "Why aren't you inside your room? Has Mr. Browser turned you out?"

"No, Mr. Salt."

A brilliant idea had just come into Michael's head. It was almost as though the Brain Sharpeners had put it there.

"I've just seen something strange on the field," he gasped. "It's the Brain Sharpeners, Mr. Salt! Don't go out there! They're after the class and Mr. Browser."

"What's that banging?" said Mr. Salt, as Mr. Browser redoubled his efforts to summon some help.

"I don't know, sir," Michael replied. Mr. Salt took a look inside the classroom and saw some of the class trying to force in the storeroom door.

"Where *is* Mr. Browser?" demanded the principal, all his old suspicions of Mr. Browser flooding back.

"I don't know," said Michael. "Perhaps the Brain Sharpeners have him. Or perhaps he's locked in the storeroom. If he doesn't come out soon, the Brain Sharpeners may go away—"

Mr. Salt pulled vainly at the handle of the classroom door. Michael watched anxiously,

103

knowing that back in his office the principal would have a master key. If he got it in time, all would be lost.

"That thing on the field looked like a pepper-pot," mumbled Michael. Mr. Salt grew tired of struggling with the door and finally looked at Michael. He didn't like being ordered about in his own school—particularly by a child. Michael had some nerve telling him not to go out on the field. How fresh!

"You're talking utter nonsense, boy," the principal declared. "I *will* go out on the field. And when I come back, having found nothing, I'll deal with you!"

10*
Back to Normal?

Mr. Salt strode off down the hall, and Michael was glad to let him go. Now there would be a further delay before the class could escape. And maybe the police would get to the field before Mr. Browser had a chance to bring the children there. They might even get there before Mr. Salt arrived.

The banging inside the classroom became frantic. It looked as though some of the boys were weakening the storeroom door. Michael moved out of sight along the hall. Then he decided to venture out to the playground and see what was happening to Mr. Salt.

A strange light was coming from the center of the field. Then the whirring sound began again. The siren of a police car wailed nearby. The whirring sound became fainter, and the fog began to thin out. Two policemen appeared, running quickly across the field.

"You there, boy!" one of them shouted.

"Yes?"

"Take me to your principal," the first policeman ordered. "Steve, you search the field in case there's anything there," he added to his partner.

Michael made a move toward the field. Then he checked himself.

"He'll be in his office," he said. "This way." He led the policeman into the school and along the hall to the principal's office. From Mr. Browser's room upstairs came a variety of banging and shouting noises. The policeman raised his eyebrows.

"Their teacher's out," explained Michael. He took the policeman to the office door and knocked. Miss Copewell came to the door.

"Miss Copewell, there's a policeman to see Mr. Salt," he announced.

"Mr. Salt is not here," she said. "He was going to look in on Mr. Browser's class."

"He's not there," said Michael.

"Then I don't know where he is," said Miss Copewell. She was used to spending a lot of time each day searching for the principal. "Would you mind waiting? I'm sure he'll be back in a minute. What's the matter?"

"Not in front of the boy," said the policeman, looking down at Michael.

"I'll go back to class," Michael volunteered.

"Good boy," said Miss Copewell.

As Michael turned the corner and climbed the stairs, he heard the assistant principal Miss Toms trying to quiet the noise from Mr. Browser's classroom.

"I'll get a cloth and break the glass," she called out.

Michael ran along the corridor.

"Don't do that, Miss Toms. I have the key!" he shouted.

"You? What are you doing with the key, Michael?"

"I went to get it, Miss Toms," said Michael, smiling at her.

"You see, I was late, and—"

"Open it up, then," she demanded, and Michael obeyed. When Miss Toms entered the room, the children moved back to their seats automatically.

"Where's Mr. Browser?" asked Miss Toms. Loud knockings on the storeroom door answered her question.

"Who has the key?" she demanded.

"I have," said Michael.

"You! But—"

For once Michael did not allow Miss Toms to finish her sentence. Instead, he went and opened the storeroom door. Mr. Browser, coat off and tie awry, shot out like a rabbit from its burrow.

"Class," he commanded, "out in line at once!"

"Where are you going?" asked the confused Miss Toms. And when Mr. Browser saw her, he also became confused.

"It's too late, Mr. Browser. They've gone!" said Michael. Mr. Browser stared at him.

"Are you sure?"

"Very sure, Mr. Browser. I heard them taking off. The fog's lifted, and there's nothing on the field."

"It's true," said Mr. Browser, looking out the window. The sun was trying to break through low clouds. Mr. Browser wiped his forehead with a handkerchief.

"Who's gone where?" demanded Miss Toms, who liked to be in control of every situation.

"Never mind, Miss Toms," said Mr. Browser with sudden firmness. "Thank you for your help. I can look after everything from now on. Class, take out your books. Sit down, Michael. Read quietly, everybody—whatever you like."

Miss Toms edged out sideways, wondering whether she ought to report all this mysterious behavior to Mr. Salt. As Michael sat down, he saw with great surprise that Spiky Jackson was reading a comic and grinning all over. His friend looked as happy as a man who's been on a desert island for months and has just seen a ship coming toward him. Michael looked around him. There was Anna Cardwell, playing quietly with a tiny doll she had found at the bottom of her desk. It had been lying untouched since the Brain Sharpeners' arrival.

"Spiky!" whispered Michael. "Shouldn't you be getting on with some work? You're wasting time with that comic."

Spiky looked up briefly and winked.

"You're a fine one to talk!" he said, and returned to his reading.

110

As Michael was congratulating himself for freeing the class from the Brain Sharpeners' spell, Miss Copewell showed up with Miss Toms and the policeman.

"Excuse me, Mr. Browser," said Miss Toms. "Has anyone seen Mr. Salt? He is said to have come this way."

Michael's hand shot up. "Mr. Salt went out on the field," he volunteered.

"I see," said Mr. Browser. "Carry on with your work, class."

Looking very grave, Mr. Browser set off for the field with Miss Toms, Miss Copewell, and the policeman.

"We had this report, called in by a child, we think—" the policeman was saying.

Five minutes later they all came back— without the principal. The policeman went to the office with Miss Toms to discuss the strange disappearance of Mr. Salt. Mr. Browser came back to the classroom just as Spiky Jackson launched the first airplane he had thrown since the Brain Sharpeners set him to work. It glided

111

through the air, then swooped and landed on Mr. Browser's desk. The whole class looked up anxiously.

"Simon Jackson," said Mr. Browser, picking up the airplane. "That's quite a well-made plane. Yes, it's the best I've seen for a while. It's nice to know you haven't forgotten how to make them. But no more, please."

Spiky Jackson's mouth opened wide. Then he grinned. "Thanks, Mr. Browser," he said.

"I think," Mr. Browser went on, "that we'll have a change of lessons this afternoon. Let's go out for some games. We haven't been outdoors for weeks because of the weather. I think you deserve a long break."

The class came back to life. Now everyone knew for sure that Mr. Browser had also escaped from the Brain Sharpeners.

"Hurray for Mr. Browser!" cried Jason Little. Everyone joined in the cheering.

"And no more homework for a while," added Mr. Browser. "Maybe we've been overdoing it a little lately."

112

Michael marveled at the smooth way in which Mr. Browser had dismissed the Brain Sharpeners from his mind—even using the weather to explain the lack of games. He decided it would be unwise to bring the subject up for a while. There were still some questions he wanted to ask, though.

Policemen in uniform were replaced later in the day by important-looking men in regular clothes. Still, there was no sign of the principal.

Late in the afternoon, a plainclothesman asked Michael some questions.

"You said you saw Mr. Salt go out on the field?"

"I saw him walking along the hall in that direction. He said he was going out on the field."

"Did he say why?"

"No," Michael answered. He had decided that unless Mr. Browser was going to talk, he would say nothing at all about the Brain Sharpeners.

That evening the parents of the children in Michael's class were surprised to discover that their sons and daughters were more interested in playing or watching television than in working. At first they were shocked and disappointed. But gradually they began to enjoy having their children back to normal—even if it did mean that they were often more trouble to them!

At school, Mr. Browser became his old self. He demanded reasonable work, but he wasn't too strict about it. Once or twice Michael approached him with the idea of asking about the Brain Sharpeners. But each time Mr. Browser sent him away because he was busy. As for Mr. Salt, the principal had disappeared without leaving a single clue behind. There were plenty of rumors, including a report in the local paper stating that maybe it was overwork which had caused Mr. Salt to vanish so completely. His wife insisted that he had been very happy at home.

Two weeks went by as though the Brain Sharpeners had never existed. Yet the continued absence of the principal was a constant reminder to Michael of all that had happened. At last he could no longer remain silent. He chose a time at the end of the school day when Mr. Browser was alone at his desk. Michael took him by surprise, doubling back from the door instead of following the other children out.

"Mr. Browser, do you think Mr. Salt will ever come back?" he asked. "If they were just sharpening up his brain for use on us, he would have been back before now, wouldn't he?"

At first Mr. Browser put on his aloof look. But

Michael's determined appearance persuaded him to talk. "I think you're right, Michael," he agreed. "I'm sure that Mr. Salt was the very sort of man they needed to develop their new territories. It wouldn't surprise me if he became a sort of Minister of Education on Planet Five—if they've managed to sharpen his brain enough. They couldn't very well let him come back after their failure with us. So they cut their losses and made off with him. They might send him back to another town to recruit other suitable people for brain-sharpening. That would probably depend on how long they're prepared to keep their space platform in its present position. If they take it back to their own galaxy, they won't be back here for hundreds of thousands of years. That's my guess."

"Then we're safe, Mr. Browser."

"I think so. But we must always be on our guard, in case they do turn up in some form or other."

But to this day there has been no sign from Mr. Salt or the Brain Sharpeners. Miss Toms was appointed principal in Mr. Salt's place, and Mr. Browser became assistant principal. The district supervisor invited by Mr. Salt arrived and found the children no smarter and no stupider than the children of most other schools. He went away saying that Mr. Salt must have been a little deranged when he disappeared.

Life returned to normal at Chivvy Chase School, and so far there's been no sign that the Brain Sharpeners have struck at any other school.

Philip Curtis

is a Deputy Headmaster of a Junior School
in England. He has written many articles for
educational journals and is the author of
short stories and plays for children.

Other Capers books by Knopf:

"I hope that Capers signal a return to the important role light, easy-to-read fiction has in getting children into the reading habit."

—DONALD J. BISSETT,
Children's Literature Center,
Wayne State University